THE GLOBAL WARMING MURDERS

FORNEY SHELL

KWE PUBLISHING, LLC

Shell, Forney. *The Global Warming Murders*

Copyright © 2025 by Forney Shell

ISBNs: 978-1-7341470-4-9 (paperback), 978-1-7341470-5-6 (e-book)

Library of Congress Catalog Number: 2025909232

Published by KWE Publishing, https://www.kwepub.com/

Cover illustration and design by Crystal Cregge, Liona Design Co.

My thanks to Dee for taking time to read the first rough draft and giving me feedback.
Thanks to Barbara Kittel for her continued support.
Thanks to Crystal Cregge of Liona Design Co. for a great cover design.
Thanks to Kim Eley and her staff at KWE Publishing for their help and suggestions.

ONE

I WAS deep in thought about how quickly things could change. I was in Washington, D.C., being driven to the White House; before that, I had been in Honduras as a guest of its government. My driver was a nice young man but a little too chipper for someone like me, having just completed an overnight flight.

My contemplation ended when he asked, "Have you ever been to the White House before?"

I responded, "I have not, nor have I ever met the president."

I fell back into my thoughts, and before I knew it, we were pulling up to the gates of the White House.

The car was approached by a well-dressed gentleman in a nice blue suit, striped tie, and white shirt. His face showed a very stern look as he said, "Identification, please."

Once he had the identification, his eyes darted back and forth between the identifications, our faces, and the interior of the car.

After returning the identifications, he produced a mirrored device and checked under the car for any explosive devices. Once satisfied there were none, a pleasant smile appeared on his face, and he motioned us through.

At the White House, I was helped from the car by a smartly dressed marine who projected both strength and respect. He said, "Good morning, sir, and welcome to the White House." With that, he held the entrance door open for me.

Inside, a man I guessed to be close to sixty met me. He said, "Good morning, Major. I hope you had a good flight. My name is Albert, and I am one of several greeters here at the White House. If you will follow me, I will take you to your appointment."

Walking through the halls, I was overcome with pride at the pictures and displays of American history.

Albert noticed my admiration of the surroundings and said, "Major, if you ever have time, I would be happy to give you a tour of the house, including its history and architecture."

I said, "That would be great. In my travels around the world, I have developed an interest in architecture, and I am impressed with the way the design of the house conveys both the beauty and strength of the nation."

After several minutes, we approached a large desk at the end of the hall. As we approached, Albert spoke to the woman behind the desk. "Good morning, Betty. This is Major Turner to see the president." To me, he said, "Major, this is Betty Jennings. She is the president's receptionist, and she will take care of you from here." He shook my hand and added, "Major, please take me up on my offer of a White House tour." And then, he left.

Betty smiled and said, "The president is looking forward to meeting you." She pressed an intercom and announced, "Mr. President, Major Kurt Turner to see you."

His response came. "Show him in."

I was directed to the Oval Office door. There, a tall, well-dressed man who appeared to be guarding the door ushered me in. The look of the Oval Office did not surprise me; I had seen it dozens of times on television and in movies. However, the feeling that engulfed me as I entered was unexpected. I felt wrapped in a blanket of historical moments. How many decisions that affected world events took place in this room? I was about to meet the most powerful man in the world, but the presence of those who preceded him seemed to hang in the air. Those men took on the responsibility of leading the nation through bright and dark days just as the nation asked them to do. Each accepted the responsibility and did their best, and the nation survived.

"Welcome to my house, Major," the president said as he stood up, came around his desk, and headed toward me with his hand extended.

I had to stop my salute mid-air and extend my hand to meet his.

He gave a small smile and said, "Sometimes, it is fun being president." He motioned to a small table and two chairs next to the wall. "Have a seat, Major."

I could see why the public liked him. The big, warm smile, the way he moved, and the way he greeted me showed he was clearly a people person. As I moved to the table, he went to his desk to obtain a thick folder and then joined me at the table.

"How was your flight, Major? I appreciate how quickly you came."

I responded, "Yes, sir, the flight was fine, sir, and when someone sends a plane, you assume they are in a hurry to talk to you."

The president replied, "I guess you are right; I seldom send a plane for a social visit. I am sure you want to know why I sent for you, so let me get right to it, and let me be very clear. I am putting together a special presidential team to study global warming and how best to respond to the natural disasters caused by global warming. It will be comprised of a small group of experts in the areas most affected by global warming. One team member will be my personal representative.

"That is where you come in, if you are willing to accept the assignment. You will act as my personal representative. You will provide security for the team and their travels. I will be assigning a member of my staff to act as team secretary. The secretary will make the team travel arrangements pending your approval. In addition to security, you will report to me directly on the team's progress or any problems the team has I might be able to help with.

"One more thing, Major, and let me be clear about this— based on your experience with disasters around the world, I want you to feel free to contribute to team discussions; however, when the team votes on an issue, you will be excluded from voting. Since you are my representative, your vote might be considered to be my opinion, and that could unbalance the vote.

"Now, before you ask, 'Why me?', let me answer it for you. I assure you, I looked at many candidates, and picking one was like selecting a diamond from a collection of gems." As he spoke, he patted the folder he had removed from his desk. "Not surprisingly, your father was in that group. Your father's time as a professor of climatology at the University of Arizona established his reputation as an expert in the field. He is also well known for his leadership ability.

"You and your father have many of the same leadership strengths. You have a solid background in climatology and are known for your leadership skills. You also have several attributes the other candidates do not. Your master's degree in national and international law with a minor in climatology is a big factor. But the deciding factor was your overseas experience in the last four or five years. Traveling with the military police unit and helping other nations with global warming disasters counted for a lot. That gives you a unique outlook on this problem.

"That's about it," said the president. "I hope I have made the assignment clear. Is it safe to assume you will take the assignment?"

Despite my head reeling from the magnitude of what had been offered and the career possibilities, I managed to say, "Yes, sir; I will."

The president shook my hand and said, "Welcome aboard. I want to get started right away, so I have arranged for everyone to meet here this evening at 5:30 for dinner and introductions. I will make brief introductions, review the purpose of the team, and explain my expectations."

TWO

UPON ARRIVING at the White House, I was shown directly to the dining room. I was surprised to learn it was managed by the U.S. Navy's culinary operations. The well-appointed room had a warm and relaxed atmosphere. There were three smartly dressed waiters in attendance. They wore waist-length black jackets, white shirts, and black bow ties. Their pants were black with a satin stripe running down both sides. The waiters took drink orders, delivered them, and then stepped back out of the way.

There were two people already there, and I assumed them to be team members. One I did not know but recognized from the media was Dr. Suzan Sanders, a well-known zoologist and animal activist. She was credited with single-handedly bringing several species of bison from the edge of extinction. I remembered newspaper articles noting that she was in her early forties. She was well dressed and, I would add, not unattractive. She looked quite robust with clear eyes and broad shoulders, standing straight and tall. She was wearing a business suit, which I assumed was not her regular working attire.

The other individual I had met when, at my father's invitation, he lectured at the University of Arizona. He was Howard Dobson, a well-respected professor and climatologist.

Just as I was introducing myself to Dr. Sanders and reintroducing myself to Professor Dobson, President Woodson entered the room. He was accompanied by seven individuals whom I assumed were the balance of the team. Four of the seven looked average, the kind of people you might expect to meet while walking down the street. The other three stood out from the group.

The first was a man with an unkempt look. He presented a slight, hunched-over stance, a frail appearance, and a wrinkled suit. When he looked in my direction, it was as if he was not seeing me at all, as if his mind was in another room, thinking strange thoughts. I was to learn later that he was Dr. Edward Milton, a well-respected entomologist.

The second was a very attractive young lady of about twenty-nine years of age. She was maybe five feet, four inches tall. Her hair was bobbed and a beautiful auburn color. She wore a white satin-looking blouse with a red calf-length skirt. From what I could see, her calves were smooth—not too skinny, not too muscular—just smooth. She was not large-breasted but extremely well proportioned. She wore shoes with three-inch heels that I suspected were to compensate for her height rather than make a fashion statement. She had beautiful green eyes that drew me in even at a distance. She stood beside and slightly behind the president.

I thought I recognized the third person as a U.S. senator, but I was not sure. He had the look of a Hollywood leading man— tall and square-jawed with wavy black hair and a dynamic smile.

My attention toward the three was broken by the president's action. He motioned for everyone to be seated, and the waiters quietly disappeared.

Then, the president began, saying, "I have yet another meeting this evening, so my time with you is limited; therefore, let me begin. Everyone was advised on the purpose of the team. I will do a brief review as I introduce the team members so you may better understand the skills and training that they bring to the group."

After each review, the president asked that we raise our hands to identify for the group the person whom he was introducing.

The president said, "I will start with the young lady on my right. Her name is Sara Colleen. She holds a few jobs here at the White House, and I am adding one more. She will be the clerical assistant to this team. In addition to providing secretarial functions, she will make your travel arrangements and obtain research assistants as needed.

"On the other side of me is a man not on the team but very interested in the team's work. He is Senator Richard Noland of the Senate Committee on Environmental Protection. He will follow the work of the team very closely.

"Next, let me move to the person in the room whom I am sure everyone is wondering about. That would be Major Kurt Turner. Major Turner is a member of a special group of military police who travel the globe assisting other nations dealing with natural disasters, many of which are caused by global warming. His unit only goes where invited and assists with traffic control, theft of relief supplies, and crowd control as needed following natural disasters. Major Turner's real hands-on experience with disasters, many caused by global warming, will be of value to the team. In addition, the major will be my contact with the team. He will keep me up to date on the progress of the team and relay to me any needs the team might have with which I could assist."

The president continued, "Seated at the table next to the

major is Mr. Richard Weston, who is well known for the accuracy of his predictions of future trends based on new and current technology. For example, what new and different jobs will exist in the future? Which states will expand or sink based on current relocation patterns?

"Next to Richard is renowned zoologist Dr. Suzan Sanders. Also at that table is Mr. William Sterns, chairperson and CEO of Alliance Auto, the largest automobile manufacturer in the United States. He has committed to converting all of Alliance's manufacturing plants to all-electric car production within the next five years. I have read that the conversion will cost well into the multi-millions, but Mr. Sterns believes it to be a major solution toward reducing carbon emissions."

I took note that Mr. Sterns was an impressive figure. He stood at a little over six feet tall with wide shoulders and graying temples and was impeccably dressed in a dark gray suit with small blue pinstripes. He wore a white shirt, a red handkerchief, and a matching tie. Since he had no apparent problem walking, I assumed the gold-headed cane he carried was no more than a fashion accessory. The president was correct in saying that, as a well-known industrial leader, Mr. Sterns gave the team the advantage of connecting with many other national industrial leaders. Also seated at that table was Professor Edward La Mount, a well-known ethicist.

The president continued, "Finally, at the next table by himself is Dr. Edward Milton, one of the world's leading entomologists, who resides in South America and is currently doing research on a spider important to humans but endangered by climate change. That completes the introductions.

"Now, I would like to move on to my expectations for you as a group, and afterward, I hope you spend the evening enjoying your dinner. Tomorrow, I would like you to return to this conference room. Then, you can spend more time learning about each other's in-depth attitudes and research on global warming. At tomorrow's meeting, I expect that you will accomplish at least three things: select a leader; set a meeting for the following month; and set an agenda for the team. "This is May, and I would like to present a progress report to Senator Noland by the end of August. Having said that, I must really run, but all of you have my deepest appreciation, and anything the team needs, just let me know."

With that, the president and the senator were gone, and the waiters magically reappeared.

THREE

FOLLOWING THE PRESIDENT'S EXIT, Miss Colleen moved from the president's group to sit next to me at my table. Once seated, she handed me a manila envelope and said, "The president asked me to give this to you."

I was curious to open it but decided to wait until I placed my dinner order, which was different from everyone else's. Since I had been out of the country for so long, all I wanted was a cheeseburger and French fries.

Upon completing my order, I opened the envelope and was pleasantly surprised at its contents. As promised, the president had arranged a car and new quarters for me. Both made me happy: the car because it was an unmarked civilian car and the quarters because they were right in Washington, D.C., at Fort McNair.

The fort was the third oldest army post in service. During the War of 1812, the British troops burnt down most of the fort, but it was later rebuilt. By 1860, a large civilian population manufactured ammunition in its arsenal. At that time, the fort also included a military hospital. In 1865, after being found guilty by a military tribunal, four conspirators in the Lincoln assassination were hanged in the fort's courtyard. Just being stationed there sort of made you part of history. Today, the fort is home to the Armed Forces Industrial College and National War College, as well as the headquarters for the U.S. Army Military District of Washington. If I had time, I thought I might be able to sit in on some classes. *With some of the best tactical military minds in the country surrounding me, I should learn something.*

During dinner, after she gave me permission, I began calling Miss Colleen "Sara" and discussing her role on the committee.

I said to Sara, "Please tell the president how pleased I am with his selection of my new duty station."

I enjoyed the conversation as well with Mr. Weston and Dr. Steward, both seated at my table.

Following dinner, I wandered around the room, introducing myself to other members of the team. I deliberately went and sat with Dr. Milton, who had been sitting alone the whole time.

I said, "Dr. Milton, you should come and sit with the rest of the team."

His forehead wrinkled, his eyes narrowed, and with anger in his voice, he replied, "I despise one of the team members and prefer to stay as far away from him as possible."

His answer took me by surprise, and I asked who the team member was. "It is Professor La Mount and his radical thinking on global warming. When it comes to global warming, he is as dumb as a carload of monkeys. His ideas will endanger my precious spiders."

I had heard that La Mount had a different view on global warming than most but had no idea it rose to such a level of hate as expressed by Dr. Milton. I asked, "Will you be able to contribute to the team feeling the way you do?"

He responded, "The president is doing the right thing, and I will contribute my knowledge to the cause and do my best to do away with La Mount's input."

After a period of socializing, we all agreed to meet at the White House the next morning at 10:10. I asked Sara to show me to the office the president had arranged for me. It was small but efficient with a desk, chair, computer, and phone—not the Oval Office but an office at the White House. I never could have imagined such a thing. Sara showed me to my car, and I headed for my new quarters and a good night's sleep.

FOUR

EVERYONE ARRIVED BACK at the White House by 10:10 the next morning and sat around the conference table, ready to begin at 10:20.

The room was very impressive. The walls were a light wood paneling, and in the middle of the room was a highly polished oak table that could seat twenty. At the head of the table was a tabletop lectern. I could not help wondering how many important decisions had been made at that very table. For a moment, my memory took a step back as the smell of furniture polish filled the room as it had in my childhood home.

Once seated, the group set about electing a leader. It went quicker than I would have imagined. I think because he was a climatologist, the team elected Professor Dobson.

The professor said, "Since I'm going to lead this group, I would like to know a little more about the group. Let us each take a turn describing our thoughts on global warming and how our work is related. I believe the major's role is most easily explained, so I will ask him to go first."

I stood up and began, "I believe global warming is real, but I'm not sure how much is man-made. I say that because each year, global warming increases faster than man's activities. If man's activities were the sole cause of warming, the two things should be proportional. Related to my job, I have seen many disasters wholly or partly related to warming. There have been fires, floods, and famine, many related in one way or another to global warming. It is surprising how quickly people turn lawless when food shortage is concerned, and that is when I step in. Before the next person speaks, I want to say that I look forward to working with each of you. Thank you for your attention."

Looking around, everyone had a smile on his or her face. Even Dr. Milton seemed in a better mood.

The next to speak was Miss Colleen. She said, "I am not a scientist, and until this group, my job at the White House gave me no inside information on the warming situation. I do know the president added global warming updates to his daily briefing. My thoughts on global warming are those of the average citizen. They give me great concern. Based on what I read and hear on the television, I have concerns about the disasters that may come in the future."

After Miss Colleen, it was Mr. Sterns' turn. Mr. Sterns, unlike the first two speakers, rose from his seat, walked to the front of the room, and stood beside the lectern. I noted he did not hide behind it like many speakers. Based on years of listening to high-ranking military officers, I knew this was usually a sign of a self-assured individual with great power.

After satisfying himself that he had everyone's attention, he began, "When I think of this group, I think of it as a working committee rather than just a team, as the president calls it. Forgive me if I refer to it as the committee. President Woodson will not mind.

"I believe completely in man-made warming, and I believe we need to start action to correct it now. I believe carbon emissions are one of the major causes of the Earth's ozone layer depletion, and gas-powered cars are a major source of carbon emissions. That is why I have committed my company, Alliance Automobile Company, the largest in the world, by the way, to produce only electric vehicles by the end of the next five years. I have committed many millions of dollars to make that happen. I am so pleased with the progress the company is making in that direction.

"For our next meeting, I invite everyone to Alliance's plant to see how we are converting to all-electric auto production. I will pick up the tab for everyone to attend our committee's meeting next month at our plant. Now that I have made that announcement, let me invite our next speaker to the podium, the attractive Suzan Sanders."

When Dr. Sanders took her place at the podium, she began by saying, "I thank Mr. Sterns for that introduction; it was what I might have expected." The sarcasm in her remark was obvious, and she looked directly at him as she said it. Dr. Sanders explained, "My work involves research on helping animals survive changes in their environment. I work through my own foundation, which is funded through several private trusts. I have two laboratories, one in this country and one in Brazil. I split my time between the two. My husband is a statistician for the foundation and spends his time in the U.S. lab. When my husband runs the numbers generated by my research, it becomes apparent that global warming is affecting the environment and even the survival of many animals."

Next in turn was climatologist Professor Dobson. I do not think his opinion surprised anyone. I was not surprised because I had heard him discuss his feelings about global warming with my father on several occasions.

When he spoke on the subject, his vision became focused, and his voice became strong and went up in volume. He said, "I am a firm believer in the planet's warming. The ocean currents are shifting, and the seasons are shifting in time and intensity. I also believe there is an alteration in weather patterns around the world. For those reasons, I am in favor of action to reverse the situation."

The next speaker was the ethicist, Professor Edward La Mount. I was interested in hearing what he had to say for a couple of reasons. First, I was interested in how he would define his contribution to the team second, what was it about his opinion that caused him to be so disliked by Dr. Milton.

La Mount started by saying, "Let me explain what I think the job of an ethicist is." As he said that, he seemed to morph into a teacher. His posture changed, and he started asking questions, starting with phrases like, "Does anyone know?" or "What do you think?"

"The job of the ethicist is to help people think through a problem and come up with the most moral solution. That does not mean that the ethicist is pure of thought and character." Even while saying it, Professor La Mount projected an air of superiority. He continued, "It does mean they have spent years studying the religions of the world, the great philosophers of the world, and the societies in which the ethicist functions. Their job is to act as a resource in decision-making.

"Let me give you an example of how that might work within this team. Let us imagine there is a valley where the water supply has dried up because of the heat. That means crops are dying. There is a dam nearby which could be opened to flood the valley. That would provide water for the crops and later food for the people, but it would also flood the valley and destroy people's homes. My job would be to enter the discussion and help look at all the moral issues before a decision is made.

"Now, about my feelings on global warming. I am afraid my thoughts are slightly different from the rest of the team's. Correctly and completely defining a problem is the surest way to solve it. I am not sure we have done that in the case of global warming. Trying to solve the problem without all the facts is like walking through a maze blindfolded. When did global warming start, and what was the temperature the day before? Was the temperature the day before the ideal Earth temperature? I think answers to these questions are critical before we start looking for a solution. Picking a number would only be slightly better than having no number.

"Suppose we were able to reverse the warming. Without knowing where it started, we would have no idea where to stop the reversal. We could go past the ideal point and start global cooling. Has anyone even considered ways to slow down and stop the reversal? That is the only way we could return to the starting point, assuming we knew what that was. If we started global cooling, would the results be the opposite of global warming? Would there be more polar bears, fewer insects, and less pollination? For these reasons, I believe the world should slow down on a search to stop global warming until it can answer the questions I have raised. I think this team should devote its effort to how best to respond to natural disasters caused by global warming." With that, Professor La Mount left the lectern and took his seat.

There was absolute silence for the next minute or so, followed by a rush of conversation. Despite the noise of so many voices, Dr. Milton arose and went to the lectern. Contrary to his normal demure self, he was clearly angry. His face was red, and his fists were clenched.

He began to speak without waiting for the conversation to die down. "La Mount is an idiot," he said. "La Mount has no idea what he is talking about. My spiders can't wait for more studies."

With the mention of his spiders, he calmed down slightly, but not by much. He went on to say, "My work is with insects, and, currently, I am devoted to working with the African jumping spider. This species produces a very deadly venom. When chemically treated, it becomes the only known treatment for several serious medical conditions.

"The mating season of this spider occurs when the temperature is in a very specific range. Global warming has caused the temperature to stay above that range, resulting in a reduction in the jumping spider population. I have set up a small desktop environment in my lab. There, the temperature is maintained for spider breeding. However, it only accommodates a small number of spiders— certainly not enough to preserve the species or produce the amount of venom needed to produce the volume of serum needed. Asking my spiders to wait while some dreamer tries to figure out how this all started is ridiculous." With that, he grabbed his notes, which he never used, and with an angry stride, returned to his seat.

We took a fifteen-minute restroom and coffee break. When we returned, Mr. Sterns stood and announced, "I have been speaking to the committee chairman and can reiterate my offer to have next month's meeting at my car factory in Arizona, as the chairman has accepted. My company owns a small hundred-room hotel to house our top customers and partners when they are at the plant. You will each have a room there, and I will provide each of you with one of our new electric cars to drive while there."

Our chairman rose and said, "The president indicated he would like to have results quickly, so I suggest at the next meeting we focus not on what causes natural disasters and how to prevent them but rather on the needs of the people caught in the disasters and how best to meet those needs. Let us come prepared with ideas and suggestions on that issue. If you have any examples, bring them. I now pronounce the meeting closed."

The members of the team left and headed back to their regular jobs. I stayed long enough to jot off a letter to the president about the first two sessions and the plans for the next session. I had not wasted time in finding out how to get to Miss Colleen's desk. When I located it, I dropped off the letter to the president with a sticky note, asking Miss Colleen to deliver it to the president, and then I left the White House.

FIVE

IT WAS EARLY EVENING, and I was not ready to return to base, so I decided to visit one of my favorite D.C. haunts, a restaurant named Michael's located a few blocks from the White House. One thing about Michael's was that it never seemed to change. When the whole world was off balance, you could go to Michael's, and everything appeared normal again.

When I entered, it was exactly as I remembered. The dining room had an elegant but warm feel to it. The walls were dark wood paneling with a rich glow created by sconces on each panel. The booths and chairs were red leather and very comfortable. My favorite hangout was the bar, which was a separate area, but it maintained the same elegant appearance. It contained a few tables and several booths, with the center focus on the wonderful bar. The bar itself was a work of art—quite long, made of highly polished mahogany, and sporting an old-fashioned brass foot rail. Upon entering, that is exactly where I headed. I ordered and received my favorite beer. I sat there, enjoying my beer and basking in the warmth of fond memories.

The side door opened, and Mike, the owner, walked through. Mike is one welcoming and happy guy. He is Italian and very good-natured. The good nature is a little surprising, considering the rough-and-tough neighborhood where he grew up. Two things he loves: cooking and eating his cooking. He is about five foot seven and barrel-chested, with the barrel shape starting to take over the rest of his appearance.

I called, "Hey, Mike."

He looked at me for a minute with non-recognition. Then, the sun broke from behind a cloud as a smile spread across his face, and he said, "Sargent Turner, it's been a long time." He came over quickly, and we shook hands and shoulder-bumped. The shoulder bump told me he was as solid as ever.

I said, "It has been a while, and it is *Major* Turner now."

He responded, "I knew you and the army were a good match. Let me get you that next beer." He walked behind the bar and handed me a cold one. "I always enjoyed you showing up because you had so many interesting stories and were always the gentleman except that one time. Do you remember when that fight started at the far end of the bar? You got off your stool, went over there, put a couple of your martial arts moves on the two guys, and walked them out. It was an impressive display and very much appreciated."

With elbows resting on the bar, Mike and I revisited old times. We reminisced for quite a long time, and then I headed back to the base.

The upcoming team meeting focusing on the needs of the people caught in global disasters gave me plenty of homework between now and then. I had the advantage over the other team members by being stationed in Washington. Washington is one of the world's news and information centers. That gave me access to government and news agency records of natural disasters not available in other locations. I also planned to use the records at the war college. I knew their records were based on disasters caused by war, but the needs of the populations caught in those combat situations should have been the same.

As I suspected, this research kept me very busy until our next meeting. I was right about the war college. I spent several days there with old newspapers and military reports spread out over a table as I studied needs following the disasters of war. The librarians were helpful, occasionally interrupting my thoughts to bring me articles they thought would be of value to my research.

SIX

THE NEXT TEAM meeting was in the middle of September at the Alliance plant outside of Phoenix. I think we were all glad it was in September because the summer in Arizona had been the hottest in years.

I arrived a day early and was met by Mr. Sterns' head of security, Mr. Jason Aba. The name reminded me of the famous singing group, Abba, from Sweden. He looked like a head-of-security guy. He was about six feet, three inches tall, and he spoke with a slight foreign accent. He was well-built and had a flattop haircut. The way he walked and carried himself indicated some kind of military background. He was attentive but all business. No smile accompanied his strong but distant-feeling handshake.

He showed me to one of several electric cars provided to the team by Sterns. It was the Pacer model, which was the only electric car in full production by Alliance. It came in two versions—the Pacer and the Luxury Pacer. We were all supplied with the Luxury Pacer, and I will say that it was impressive. It had very comfortable seats covered in cream colored, smooth-to-the-touch leather. Of course, it smelled like a new car. The electric car was very quiet, and the Pacer sound system made the car sound more like a concert hall than a car. The onboard computer had already been programmed with directions to the Alliance hotel.

When I started to drive away, I was jerked to attention by the unexpected acceleration. With an electric car, there is no delay between pressing the pedal and going, and that takes a little getting used to.

After a short drive, I arrived at the hotel. The outside looked like most average hotels, but the inside was a very different story. It was clearly designed to put the fleet-car-buyer in a mode to spend his company's money. The experience upon entering the lobby was humbling if nothing else. It was cavernous and composed of steel beams painted white. The beams supported huge sheets of glass. Opposite the entrance was the reception counter with a single receptionist and one security guard.

The one thing in the lobby that grabbed your attention was behind the reception desk, and that was a large oil painting of Mr. William Sterns. Just in front of the check-in counter were several armchairs to use when waiting your turn.

During my check-in, the receptionist pointed out several features of the hotel. "To your left is our coffee shop, open twenty-four hours with complimentary breakfast, served from 6:00 AM until 11:00 AM. To the right, behind the monogrammed glass doors, is our formal dining room. Just off the entrance is our lounge. Down the hall is the exercise room, and past that is the pool. If requested, we will provide you with a physical trainer for your stay. The second floor is home to our business center and conference rooms. Those rooms are equipped with audio and visual equipment at no charge." The receptionist said, "Mr. Sterns asked that I tell you he is out of town until late this evening but will be happy to greet everyone in the morning."

As I headed to the elevator, my senses were engulfed by the aroma of fresh flowers and the cooling pastel colors throughout the lobby.

Midday saw the arrival of a few other team members, and by evening, everyone was at dinner. The food was a delight to the eye with wonderful swirls of colors in an amazing presentation.

After dinner, we all ended up in the bar for drinks and friendly conversation except for Dr. Milton, who, it turned out, did not drink, and I was sure he was not interested in sharing conversation with some members of the team. Around 10:30, we all headed to bed so we would be rested and ready for a long meeting the next day.

The next morning, we all returned to the lobby, where the receptionist greeted us and said she would notify Mr. Sterns that we were there. A few moments passed and Mr. Sterns entered through a side door.

He looked as put together and in charge as I remembered. He said he wanted to show us the plant before we sat down for the meeting, and off we went with Mr. Sterns in the lead.

Upon entering the factory, we left the world of quiet strength and entered the world of mechanical sights and sounds. There were the sounds of presses forcing metal to conform to the desired shape. There were the sights of sparks and flashes of welders as they fused metal to metal, and the smells of well-oiled machines at work filled the air.

We first toured the production line for the gas-powered cars, and it was quite impressive but not as impressive as the electric car production line, which we toured next. Alliance made four different models of electric cars. The Pacer was mid-sized and the only one in full production as an all-electric car. The other three were the luxury model Metro-Glide, the large Metro, and the compact Urban. The production line was moving along smoothly.

Mr. Sterns told us, "If a mistake is detected, the whole line stops while it is fixed. The workers receive a bonus based on daily production numbers, so when the line stops, everyone on the line knows a mistake was made and that it is costing them money. That means everyone has a reason to reduce errors."

In the next building, two of the truck models were in production; both were gas-operated. The all-electric truck was in production in the same building as the Pacer. That area was next; it was where we could tell Mr. Sterns felt the proudest. It was truly something to behold. The process was ninety percent automated and produced cars and trucks at an amazing rate. I now understood the huge amount of money Sterns was investing by going all-electric.

By then, it was lunchtime, so we went to the conference room, which was already set up for us. Mr. Sterns had arranged a buffet, and we served ourselves from an eye-catching array of meats, salads, and desserts.

Following lunch, we were shown to the restrooms, and when we returned, the food and dishes had been removed and ready for our meeting. The room was clearly designed for such meetings. Each position at the table had its own speakerphone. A staff assistant placed notepads and pencils at each location.

With a wave of his hand, Sterns dismissed the assistant, and the meeting began.

Once the meeting started, it was obvious that everyone had done his or her homework. All had pictures and videos of natural disasters, which, in part, could have been caused by global warming.

Identifying the human needs after the disasters was the easy part. The difficulty was ranking the needs in order of importance. We quickly realized that there were common human needs after all the disasters, but the ranking of those needs depended on factors unique to the disaster. The team ended up listing the types of disasters. On that list were floods, droughts, fire, hurricanes, tornadoes, earthquakes, and land- and snowslides. Under each item, we listed a series of questions to be asked of each disaster. The questions were designed to help identify the human needs. They included questions such as, "Were homes destroyed? What was the sanitary condition? Were food supplies destroyed? Were rescues required?"

Once completed, and with a mixture of smiles, head nods, and relaxing shoulders, we all signed the list—except Professor La Mount. He signed the list but added a footnote. His footnote read, "I agree with the list but do not agree with the approach. I think the team should be focused on establishing the proper climate for which to aim and the ways to get there."

We agreed to meet again in three weeks with an agenda to look at the available resources to meet the human needs, as per our list. The team voted to meet next in Aspen, Colorado. It was ski season, and I think some were looking forward to a government-funded working vacation. Dr. Milton was pleased because one of the laboratories that processed spider venom into usable human form was in Denver. By meeting in Aspen, he could bring several vials of unprocessed venom and drop them off in Denver on his way home.

Before heading back to Washington, I forwarded my notes to Miss Colleen to be typed and given to the president.

Back in Washington, I called the president and brought him up to date on the team's progress. I also asked if Miss Colleen could travel with the team, thus making communication quicker and more efficient. The president agreed and said he would inform Miss Colleen.

SEVEN

THE TEAM HAD AGREED to meet in Aspen on November 10 for dinner at 7:00. I arrived a little before 1:00. Getting out of the car in front of the Aspen hotel, I shivered as a gust of cold air assaulted my body. I wished I were wearing my sunglasses, as the day was clear and very bright. I understood why some of the team had arrived a day early and were already on the slopes.

I unpacked and headed for the bar to relax. The bar area offered beautiful views of the snow-capped mountains. The feeling generated by the view was in sharp contrast to the warmth and comfort of the bar area itself.

Upon entering, I saw Miss Colleen sitting at a small table off to the side of the bar. I joined her, and for the next hour or so, we had a very pleasant conversation. Her personality turned out to be as lovely as she was. Her smile, combined with her direct and indirect glances, held my attention all the while. She proved to be quite a good conversationalist on a wide range of topics. She was from Vermont, where she had attended secretarial school, and after graduation, she had gone on to get her degree in political science. This encouraged her to seek a job at the White House, where she had been for a little over five years.

She eventually excused herself, saying, "I don't ski, but I do ice skate and want to try the hotel's ice rink before dinner."

I hung out a while longer and then headed to my room. I wanted to review both my notes from prior meetings and the information I would be sharing later.

When I arrived at dinner, everyone was there except Mr. Sterns. The conversation was in full swing, not about the meeting but about ski conditions and the beauty of our surroundings.

About twenty minutes later, Mr. Sterns arrived and apologized for being late, saying, "There was a problem at the factory that needed my attention."

Following an evening of good food, a little drinking, and pleasant conversation, everyone headed to his or her room. The next day would be long, and people wanted to prepare.

The next morning, we all arrived at the conference room on time. The room was nice but a long way from what we'd had at the Alliance plant. The Alliance-style buffet had been replaced with a plate of cookies and an urn of coffee. Without the big show of hospitality, we were able to get right down to work. The chairperson reminded us that the focus of the meeting was the evaluation of resources available for the various disasters. We quickly realized the resources needed would depend on the type of disaster, and the number of resources would depend on the country where the disaster occurred. We put in a long day, and at the end, we were ready for dinner and some relaxation.

That evening, dinner was at 6:00, and everyone arrived on time except for Mr. La Mount. We decided to wait to order until he arrived. At twenty after six, we went ahead and ordered. I became a little concerned and asked the team members about Mr. La Mount.

Dr. Sanders said, "I saw him go into his room around 5:00."

After placing my dinner order, I excused myself, went to the house phone, and called La Mount's room but got no answer. After another fifteen minutes, I decided to go to his room and check on him. I knocked on the door and received no answer.

Turning the knob, I discovered the door was unlocked, and I entered, announcing myself as I did. The only light in the room was filtering through the drawn drapes. It took a minute for my eyes to adjust, but when they did, I spotted La Mount sprawled on the couch, his eyes wide and staring at the ceiling, his face distorted in a mask of pain. His hands gripped his belly as if trying to strangle something inside. I immediately went over, checked for a breath or pulse, and found neither. I notified the hotel staff, had them lock the room, and notified the police.

EIGHT

WHEN THE POLICE ARRIVED, I introduced myself, showed them my presidential letter of introduction, and asked them to keep me informed. Since Miss Sanders had seen La Mount at about 5:00 PM, there was no problem establishing the time of death.

The coroner took one look at his face, the color of his lips, and the pupils of his eyes and said, "The cause of death is mostly likely poison." He added that he would know with certainty after his examination, and if it was poison, what kind. After those remarks, he went about his business, showing no signs of concern working with a dead body.

The police detective's face showed a grimace when looking at the body. He said, "I can't help feeling a little human contact with the victim when I see they obviously died in pain."

In reviewing the crime scene, the police noted the doctor's wallet was empty of cash, and his expensive watch was missing, leaving only a shape where the sun had not left a tan. There were a few strands of hair in La Mount's hand, but the DNA test would show no matches. The police also checked La Mount's phone records during his stay and discovered two calls from U.S. Senator Richard Noland, each slightly over thirty-five minutes long. The detective noted I seemed surprised and asked if I knew about them.

I explained the senator's interest in the team but said, "I had no knowledge of the calls." In fact, I was surprised La Mount had not mentioned them.

I was allowed to sit in on the detective's interviews with the team members. Each team member was asked if he or she knew anyone who disliked La Mount and if he or she knew about the senator's phone calls. Each spoke of the great dislike shown by Edward Milton toward Mr. La Mount. No one knew of the phone calls. Everyone expressed sorrow at Mr. La Mount's death. Several people said that, even though they privately thought he was a pompous ass, he did not deserve to die like that. When the police learned that Dr. Milton was transporting poison to the laboratory in Denver, they asked him if they could see the samples.

Dr. Milton stared at the detective for a moment and then agreed, saying, "All you will find are three small, sealed vials of spider venom."

In his room, the doctor removed a small cooler from the refrigerator. From the cooler, he removed a small black plastic pouch about the size of a man's wallet. When opened, the first visual was a syringe supposedly used to fill or empty vials.

The appearance of the vials caused Dr. Milton to turn ashen white. His eyes widened, and he seemed to freeze. Two of the vials were completely full, but the third was only half full. He swore all three had been full when he packed them, and he had not touched them since.

The police confiscated the pouch and its contents. They took several pictures of the pouch, and because of potential spoilage, they sent the samples to the Denver laboratory. I was told that except for Dr. Milton, the rest of the team could return home the next day. Dr. Milton was ordered not to leave town.

The police told me, "We have enough evidence to arrest the doctor but will wait for the coroner's report and to check Dr. Milton's alibi."

I called the coroner's office to see when the report might be available. I was told it was delayed because they were trying to identify the poison. It was a rare type not normally seen in homicide cases.

That afternoon, I received a call from the police. The coroner had identified the poison as a rare spider venom. They also said they were able to verify Dr. Milton's alibi since the team could vouch for his whereabouts during the evening. The question then became if the killer was not Dr. Milton, who else knew he was carrying the spider venom?

That evening, I joined the doctor for dinner. He had arrived first, and as I approached the table, he was sitting rigid, squeezing and unsqueezing his hand while rocking slightly back and forth.

Once seated, I put the question directly to the doctor. "Other than yourself, who else knew you were transporting the spider venom?"

He identified the members of the team, the laboratory where he was taking the venom, and, of course, his assistant at his own laboratory. He had also discussed with hotel management having samples in the hotel refrigerator and asked that they alert housekeeping. The notification to housekeeping was to make sure the samples were not disturbed. I asked if those were all the people who knew, and he assured me they were.

After a few more sips of his coffee, Dr. Milton said, "Wait, there is one other person."

On the plane, he had explained to a female passenger why there had been an ice chest in the seat between them. Not wanting the cooler out of his sight, he had bought a separate seat for the cooler. I asked if he knew anything about the woman. He only said that she was staying at the same hotel as us and was going skiing for the week.

The doctor was lucky to have been having dinner with the team, thus creating a firm alibi. I say "lucky" because he was an easy target to frame. However, the theft of the wallet and watch did not fit in with an attempt to frame the doctor. It did raise the question: Would someone really kill over a small robbery? If yes, would the thief use poisoning? In addition, there remained a question of motive. As far as I knew, no one disliked La Mount enough to kill him except Dr. Milton, and he had a solid alibi.

NINE

DR. MILTON and I shared a shuttle to the airport. He departed for home a half hour before I headed to Washington, D.C. When I arrived in Washington, I went to the base to freshen up and then to the White House to brief the president. As I talked to him, his head kept moving from side to side, and he continually put his hand to his mouth as I relayed the happenings of the last few days.

I paused. We both took in a deep breath, and I began again. I told the president about the questions I wanted answers to. I said, "I will be checking on the woman Dr. Milton had talked to on the plane." I also told him, "I intended to stay in touch with the Aspen police, and I will continue looking for a motive."

The president said, "I am thankful for the update. I am sure you appreciate the shock and sadness I feel at hearing of the doctor's murder. I will direct Miss Colleen to make the arrangements for a memorial service, including working with the doctor's family to ensure a memorial befitting his service to his country." The president continued, "Let me make this clear—I want the work of the team to continue, and more than ever, I want you to remain as part of the team. I want you to continue to investigate and stay alert until we understand what's going on."

I asked the president if he knew anything about the phone conversations between Dr. La Mount and Senator Noland.

The president shook his head and replied, "I do not. The only thing I know is that the senator was impressed by La Mount's argument to slow down looking for a solution to global warming until we understood better what success would look like. The senator agreed that the team's effort to identify emergency responses to global disasters should continue."

Several days after my meeting with the president, I received a call from the Aspen police. They had received a hit on Dr. Milton's stolen credit card. A housekeeping employee from the hotel used the card to purchase gas at a local gas station. After questioning, the employee admitted to taking the card. He had gone to La Mount's room, found him dead, took the watch and contents of the wallet, and left without telling anyone. He had checked into work in plenty of time to commit the theft before I checked on La Mount. That was one mystery out of the way.

I had done some investigation and found the name of the woman Dr. Milton had met on the plane. A background check showed no prior contact. Therefore, I wrote her off as simply a random contact. I felt a little relief because that was a second question out of the way. The question of motive still stood out as large as a Saint Bernard in the kiddie pool. I decided to do a thorough background check on Dr. La Mount and see what turned up. I would start with his high school and work my way forward. He attended the Science and Technology Magnet School in Dallas, Texas. Nothing negative showed up at the high school—just the opposite. Dr. Milton was well liked and a good student, showing a talent for mathematics. He was popular with the girls and had one teenage romance that ended when he went off to attend Stanford University in California.

At Stanford, the pattern continued. Remembered as being easygoing, he had done very well as a member of the swimming team. Nowhere in my search did I find anyone who disliked the man. He graduated with a bachelor's degree in statistical analysis. After graduation, he took a job with an insurance company as an actuary. The insurance company was a little hesitant to talk about a former employee, but after some friendly conversation and assurances, they were willing to help. After a little over a year with the insurance company, he left to return to Stanford, where he earned a master's and PhD in ethics and philosophy.

After Stanford and before joining the president's team, he worked at a hospital in California and one in Washington, D.C. While in California, he did volunteer work at a prison, teaching a class in ethics and morality. The prisoners appreciated La Mount and his classes.

I started finding people who might have held a grudge only when looking at his work at the hospital. During any given week, the hospital medical staff made many critical decisions about ethical and moral issues involving their patients. Dr. La Mount's job was to give them his expert opinion on those issues. Only three cases out of the many that La Mount worked on generated anger toward him. In one case, trying to save a patient's leg could have cost the patient his life. La Mount had recommended amputating the leg. In the second case, a young pregnant wife was in a severe car accident. La Mount had recommended saving the mother, which caused the child to die. The third case was the reverse of the second. A woman in her fifties was pregnant and had tripped and fallen down a flight of stairs, suffering major brain damage. The question was whether to save the woman or the child. Only one could be saved. La Mount had recommended saving the child. In all cases, the individual losing the leg and both husbands of the pregnant women had been the ones to become angry with La Mount over his recommendations.

All incidents had occurred quite a while back, but I was able to locate and talk to the individuals. None of the three individuals still held grudges. The husband, whose wife had lost the child, showed great love for the wife he still had, and his chest swelled as he introduced the two boys whom they had gone on to have. The boy who lost his leg was living a normal life and happy to be alive. The husband of the wife whose life had been taken missed his wife but realized she would not have been the same with severe brain damage. The child saved was a beautiful daughter, who was now a vibrant part of her father's life. Since there was no one in La Mount's past who presented a motive, the motive was still a part of the mystery.

TEN

A COUPLE of weeks passed between my meeting with the president and Dr. La Mount's memorial service, so I used the time to relax. I took advantage of the base's gym to get back to my training regimen and used the firing range to help maintain my pistol skills. Miss Colleen and I spent several evenings together, which turned into several nights together. Many of those evenings started at my old haunt, Michael's restaurant. It was very relaxing and rejuvenating to taste a cold beer, feel the softness of a caring woman, and see familiar surroundings.

My relaxation ended, and I returned to the job the day I attended La Mount's memorial service. I was not surprised that it was very well attended. Dr. La Mount was liked and very active in Washington, D.C., social circles. All the team members attended the service. Each seemed to be withdrawn in their own thoughts over the events that led to them being there. I was not surprised to see Senator Noland but was to see several members of his Congressional Environmental Committee. I made a mental note to talk to them in the coming week.

As I was leaving the service, the president got my attention and asked me to stop by the White House at 2:00 PM the next day. He said, "I have something to share with you."

I headed back to base and then went to Miss Colleen's.

Arriving the next day at the White House, I was shown directly to the Oval Office. The president was there with a man I had met many times—George Harding—a reporter and opinion-piece writer for the *Washington Post* newspaper. He was well known and respected for his fieldwork covering armed conflict and natural disasters. Our broad smiles and warm greetings let the president know we were old friends. I explained I had met George several times when working on natural disasters in my role with the military police; George had covered the same disasters for his paper.

"Good," said the president. "Then you understand why I asked George to be on the team."

Putting a hand on George's shoulder, I said, "Not only do I understand, but I also agree completely with his selection."

The response was, "Let me be clear—I know he is not an ethicist, but as you know, he has a working knowledge of the results of global warming. I believe his position on the newspaper will give us fair-handed reporting to the public on our conclusions."

George and I shook hands again as I welcomed him to the team. Looking at George, I reflected on how deceiving looks can be. He stood about five feet, five inches tall, had a small frame, a smooth complexion, and a great smile. It was hard to imagine this same person going into partially collapsed buildings looking for survivors. It was also hard to envision this small-framed man lifting heavy rubble off a mother and child. When you saw him work a disaster site, you would think he was working to save his own family. He was going to be a great member of the team.

ELEVEN

IN THE NEXT day's *Washington Post*, George's column was a story about the team's work and La Mount's part in it. I assumed the president wanted to get political support for his global warming project and had asked George to write about the team. That morning, the television, radio, and national newspapers all ran the story of the team and the doctor's murder. Most read similarly, saying, "While working as part of a presidential committee to solve global warming, renowned ethicist Dr. Edward La Mount was found dead in his hotel room..."

This was the first time the public heard of our committee, and over the next few days, we received thousands of letters telling us how to solve the climate problem. In addition to the White House mailroom, my tiny office was stacked high with hundreds of letters from all parts of the country. Many were reasonable, like switching to all-electric cars or shutting down all coal-powered plants. Others were just too far out. Many thought aliens were to blame, and if we started shooting down flying saucers, the problem would go away. My favorite suggestion was simply to move the Earth farther away from the sun.

There were so many suggestions that the president gave

the team an extra staff person to handle the increased volume of mail. The extra staff person was asked to compile a list of any write-in global control suggestions that seemed to make sense. Out of several hundred, forty were worth consideration at our next meeting. Since I wanted to talk to several senators, I arranged for the next team meeting to be held in Washington.

At that meeting, we went through the forty suggestions and set aside eleven for further review. We had a little something to cheer about at that meeting. During a break between our meetings, a large forest fire had broken out in the mountains of Colorado. Our team had previously prepared a list of all federal government, National Guard, and states with water-dropping planes. These planes could scoop water from a river or lake as they flew over and could drop the water on the forest fire. Thanks to that list, the president was able to order additional planes from nearby locations. The result was getting the fire under control quicker than ever before with game-changing results.

Several days after the fire was controlled, the president stepped into my office with a cheerful and satisfied look on his face. He handed me an article clipped from the local newspaper. It was about the amount of forest acreage saved due to the list prepared by the president's global warming team.

The president said, "I have to run, but please convey my appreciation to the team," and with that, he was gone.

The team's acceptance of George Harding went smoothly. Several team members read his column regularly, and all members were interested to hear his thoughts on global warming.

We spent part of the next meeting bringing each other up to date about happenings in our lives since our last meeting. Dr. Milton was concerned that funding for his spider research might be reduced because of the negative publicity concerning his involvement in La Mount's death.

Just the opposite was true with Dr. Sanders. Her "Save the Animals Foundation" had received a large donation from a major pet food manufacturer. She could not stop bragging about what a great company they were and what wonderful products they produced.

The happiest moment came when we learned Professor Dobson and his wife had celebrated the birth of their second granddaughter. Mother and child were doing fine, and of course, the professor came to the meeting prepared with pictures of the newborn. Looking at him showing the pictures almost made believing in the possibility of a smile from ear to ear easy.

After the first hour, we were back on track, reviewing our progress and setting future goals. Before heading to base, I asked Miss Colleen to set up a meeting for me with Senator Jackson of Washington State and Senator Drake of Texas.

Over the next few days, I used the base's library to do a little research on both senators.

The following Tuesday, I met with Senator Jackson. After checking in with his administrative secretary, I was approached by a man who introduced himself as the senator's security guard. He was well-dressed and polite but all business. He said he needed to pat me down. As he began, I informed him that I had a gun in a holster under my jacket. No sooner had I said it than he went under my jacket and reached for the gun. I grabbed his wrist before he got to the gun with such force that I saw him wince in pain.

I said in a firm but soft voice, "I represent the president of the United States, and I do not give up my weapon."

He withdrew his hand and stepped aside, and I proceeded to the senator's office. The senator was not fat but on the heavy side. He had a pleasant smile and hardy handshake. I thought to myself, *I am glad I am not a baby, or I would have gotten a kiss.*

The senator said, "I read in the paper that you are part of the president's team on global warming. How can I help you?"

I replied, "I saw you at the memorial service for Professor La Mount and just wondered how you knew him."

He responded, "As you know, I am on the Senate Committee on Environmental Protection. Our committee chairman had a number of discussions with Professor La Mount about his thoughts on stopping global warming. As you may also know, La Mount thought we would be wasting time and money trying to stop or reverse the warming without knowing to what temperature we were trying to return. Our committee chairman, Senator Noland, thought enough of the doctor's thinking that he invited him to share his thoughts with the committee. He spoke to us twice—once about the need to know how to measure success in stopping and reversing the warming.

"He spoke a second time on the ethics of spending taxpayer money on something with no defined end. La Mount preferred we spend the money on controlling the effects of warming until we defined what the beginning and end of the warming looked like.

"Senator Drake, whom you may have seen with me at the memorial service, and I both agreed with his point of view. Senator Drake and I both have problems that need to be addressed now and not two years from now. The increase in temperatures is killing crops in the fields, and farmers simply cannot afford the cost to install the needed irrigation. Major cities are seeing a rise in physical violence because increased temperatures are causing shorter tempers and frustration. There are many other state problems being created by global warming that need attention now."

After a little more conversation, I thanked him for his time and told him I was heading to the congressional dining room for lunch and then on to my meeting with Senator Drake.

His eyebrow went up, and he stared for just a moment, then said, "I am about ready for lunch. Do you mind if I join you?"

I, of course, had no objection, and we headed for the congressional dining room.

Once seated in the dining room with our orders placed, Senator Jackson asked, "Do you have an appointment with Senator Drake?"

I said, "Yes; did you think I was just going to walk in?"

He said, "You may have noticed my surprise when you said you were meeting with the senator. That was because the senator's wife passed away a few weeks ago, and he has not been in the office much since then. If you have an appointment, it means he is back at work, and he needs that. Hopefully, it will help take his mind off his loss."

I asked, "How long had they been married?"

He replied, "A little over twenty years; two years ago, she and the senator took a trip to Africa to drum up business for his home state of Texas. A couple of weeks after returning, his wife came down with an unidentified illness. Hospitals and universities across the country tried to identify it, but none could. She spent the last few years on experimental and expensive drugs and treatments."

The senator was momentarily interrupted when our order arrived. Then, he continued, "Senator Drake's wife had trouble keeping food down, always had a low-grade temperature, and became weaker and weaker. She finally passed away about two weeks ago. I'm afraid Drake blames himself for taking his wife with him to Africa."

After lunch, I thanked the senator for his insight and assured him I would be respectful of the circumstances. Then, I was off to Senator Drake's office. It was a short walk, and I was welcomed by a woman I judged to be in her mid-fifties. She was well-dressed, with a warm smile and pleasant voice.

She greeted me by saying, "Good afternoon, Major. Please follow me." She stood and led me to the senator's office.

I entered and received the same kind of handshake I had received in the previous senator's office. It was firm but not too firm and made you feel like the senator was happy to meet you. It made me wonder if the senators all went to the same handshake school. Another common trait—all senators appeared well-dressed. I thought to myself, *A men's clothing store on Capitol Hill would be a moneymaking second career.*

I was surprised to see the senator was quite short, about five feet, five inches tall. He had a full head of brown hair with no signs of gray, and he appeared to be in good shape. I had read that he had one shoulder lower than the other, but it was not visible. I guess his suit had been tailored to compensate. There was, however, sadness that hung over him like a dark cloak. I expressed my sorrow at his loss and apologized for intruding at such a time.

He seemed to retreat in thought for a moment, then thanked me for my concern and said, "Life must go on."

I asked him the same questions I had asked the other senator and got very similar answers. He agreed with La Mount that there were problems caused by warming that needed a solution before trying to reverse the warming. I thanked him for his time and left.

TWELVE

WHEN I RETURNED to the barracks, I had three phone messages waiting for me. The first was to let me know my dry cleaning was ready. The second was from Miss Colleen, asking for a call back. The third call was unexpected and a complete surprise. It was from my other boss, General Browning, commander of the military police. I had never spoken to the man and wondered how concerned I should be that he was calling. Wisdom told me to return the call right away. When I did, I got the general's aide, who said the general was away from his desk. He would try to locate him and get back to me. Ten minutes later, he called back with the general on the line.

When I said hello, a very strong voice on the other end said, "Hello, Major; this is General Browning. How are you this evening?"

I said, "Doing well, sir, thanks for asking! It's a pleasure to speak to you, sir."

He responded, "Let me get right to the point of my call. First, at the request of the president, you have been permanently assigned to the president's staff. Congratulations! The president thinks highly of your contributions.

"Secondly, with your new assignment, your unit needs someone with the rank of major assigned to it. I understand the person we are promoting to that position is an old friend of yours, Captain Jack Burton. I called to see if you would like to personally present the promotion to Captain Burton."

Jack was an old friend of mine, and I knew he was a great choice. I replied, "I would be pleased and honored to do it, sir. You are correct when you say Captain Burton is a friend. We both took basic training at Fort Leonard Wood, and he graduated from the police training camp following me. Over the years, there were many times when he had my back in dangerous situations."

The general said, "I am glad you can do the honors. The ceremony is in two weeks at Fort Leonard Woods and starts at 2:00 PM. Keep up the good work, and have a good evening."

Then, the general was gone. I sat there for a few minutes, thinking about what had just happened. Then, I realized I needed to return the call to Miss Colleen.

Miss Colleen said the president wanted to set up a meeting with me. I also wanted a meeting with him. I was upset that the president would have me permanently reassigned without consulting me first. I did not mind the reassignment. I just thought courtesy demanded that I be consulted before it happened.

I had Miss Colleen set up a meeting with the president for the day after next. I thought if I were to tell the president of the United States he had overstepped, I should take a day to figure out the best way to approach the issue.

While I had her on the phone, I advised Miss Colleen of my trip to Fort Leonard Wood. I told her the days I would be there and asked her to clear my schedule for those dates and mark them on my calendar. I also told her about an airfield at the Fort that operated commercial flights and asked her to make me round-trip reservations.

I thought about the best way to approach the president. I did not want to say the wrong thing or give the wrong impression. I wanted him to know I was pleased with the assignment. It was just the way it was done that did not sit well. I finally realized there was no good way. So, when we met, I opened the discussion head-on.

I said, "Mr. President, I just learned of my new assignment as a permanent member of your staff. Let me say that I am pleased and honored by your faith in me. I look forward to being of service in any way I can. However, I am concerned over one phase of your action. I feel I should have been consulted before the decision was made. I realize you had no requirement to consult me before the decision; after all, you are the commander-in-chief.

"Let me explain my thinking. You know my record, so you know I graduated with a master's degree and could have gone into private sector employment with a nice salary. Yet, I chose a military career. Then, once in, I applied to join the military police. That was the career I chose for myself. You appear to have arbitrarily changed my chosen career path with no concerns about my thoughts on the matter. Based on the working relationship I thought we had, I would have expected to be consulted."

The president registered a faint look of hurt momentarily. Then, he spoke. "There was no disrespect intended, and I apologize if there was. Of course, you are right; I should have talked to you first. I had intended to do it, but before I could, a team from the Pentagon came for a meeting, and your general was one of the members. I took the opportunity to arrange your reassignment at that time with the intention of letting you know later. Apparently, your commander let you know first, and you felt left out. That was not my intention; again, I apologize."

I repeated, "I am very pleased with the assignment." I told him one result of the whole thing was a friend of mine was getting promoted to major and taking over my old unit. I advised him I would be taking off for a few days to present the promotion to my friend.

He said, "I am pleased it has worked out so well for your friend; when you see him, give him my congratulations."

THIRTEEN

LATER, when it came time to fly to Fort Leonard Wood, I was more excited than I imagined I would be. I was heading back to where it all began. Fort Leonard Wood was one of several large basic training bases around the country. After basic training, if you were to become an engineer, military policeman, or part of the chemical corps, you would get training at Fort Leonard Wood. During World War II, the base was used to intern Italian and German prisoners of war. I felt I was heading back into memories, both good and bad, with good friends being the best of the good.

The flight went well. When I arrived, I picked up a car at the motor pool and headed to the base command center. Once there, I was assigned a place to stay and directed to the most likely place to find Captain Burton. Then, I was off to find my friend. I was told he would be observing his men at the pistol range, and that is where I headed. I drove to where my memory directed, but my memory and things had changed. I ended up in the wrong place and was redirected to the proper location. The pistol range was in a building next to the outdoor rifle range. When I entered, I instantly saw the captain in the glass-enclosed observation booth. He was easy to spot since the booth was raised slightly above the firing line. That allowed the range master and observers to simultaneously see the firing line and the targets.

It took a few minutes before he looked in my direction, but when he did, his whole person seemed to light up. He quickly found a lieutenant to take his place and came to greet me. We shared a couple of big bear hugs and slaps on the back before heading to the officer's club. Once there, we settled in for lots of good reminiscing and one or two beers, maybe three, four, or more.

The next morning, despite being a little foggy from the night before, I put on my dress uniform and headed to the office where the promotion presentation would take place. The captain was in his dress uniform and looked very sharp. Presenting the promotion made me feel very good. It was truly satisfying to see one of my men reach the same rank as me. It was also satisfying to know that my old unit would be in capable hands.

Following the ceremony, there was a small party in the barracks, which I attended. There, I saw many of my old friends. I had to take much kidding because I was working for the president. Many guys asked if I could have the president restation them in Hawaii or the coast of Italy. Some wanted to see if I could get their promotions pushed ahead. It was all in good fun, and all had a good time.

The next morning, Major Burton and I met for breakfast. I shared my thoughts on the personnel in the unit and what made a good unit.

Since it was my last day on base, the major and I decided to have some fun. We first went to the gym for a little boxing. When it came to martial arts, Major Burton could never beat me, but boxing was just the opposite. His hands were much faster than my ability to block. One minute, his left glove was next to his chest, and the next, it was in my face. Boxing with Jack was one way to get red, rosy cheeks quickly, and Jack loved it. Next, we went to the high-speed auto chase track and took turns pursuing and being pursued.

Come 7:00 PM, it was time to take my flight back to Washington. A handshake, another big bear hug, and I said goodbye to a good friend and headed home.

Arriving at the airport in Washington, I headed to baggage claim and was met with a pleasant surprise. I had planned to pick up my bag and take a cab to the base for a good night's sleep. Instead, Miss Colleen was waiting for me and drove me to her place. We had a late dinner and an early breakfast. I will say, in comparison to an active night with Miss Colleen, sleep is overrated.

Back at the base, I took a shower, put on fresh civilian clothes, and called the Aspen police. I was curious to know if there was anything new in the La Mount case, and there was nothing. The Aspen police reminded me that when a crime was committed at a resort hotel, all the possible suspects except for the resort staff would leave and scatter across the country. That made follow-up investigation close to impossible. They assured me it was still an open case and said they would keep me informed.

My next call was to Senator Noland's office. I wanted to talk to him about his meetings with La Mount. His secretary answered and said the senator was in a committee meeting; she would advise him that I called and get back to me. Shortly after, she called back and said, "The senator is going on a fact-finding trip to Korea over the next two weeks, and when he returns, he would be happy to call and set up a time for a meeting."

Following the call, I headed to the base library to use their computer. With the War college located at the base, the library was very well stocked and very convenient. I needed to do my homework for the next team meeting.

At the next meeting, the entire team was excited; we had been invited to an international meeting on global warming in Paris. Dr. Dobson, the team's climatologist, would discuss his work on predicting drought and rainfall patterns for the next ten-year period.

FOURTEEN

MY ONE THOUGHT when arriving at the Paris hotel was that whoever picked it knew how to pick a hotel. The lobby was very plush but done in good taste. It was large and well-appointed. The rooms were a good size with a separate working area containing a desk and computer.

Various team members flew in from different locations, and I did not see them until that evening at the cocktail reception. There was plenty to drink, and the hotel kept the beautifully prepared hors d'oeuvres coming.

After the cocktail hour, we enjoyed an exceptionally delightful dinner. Each large group attending the conference was seated at its own table. Smaller groups shared a table. My team took up an entire table and accommodated two additional strangers. We learned they were from NASA and were there to announce NASA's launch of a new satellite. Both men were young and excited to be in Paris and about the new satellite. The satellite was to circle the Earth and measure the industrial sites that were producing large amounts of carbon emissions. This would lead to identifying the biggest polluters needing corrective action.

The cocktail party and dinner both went well, with the conversation switching between the mundane and concerns over global warming.

On the second night of the convention, the entire team went out together on the town. Several members had been to Paris before, and they acted as our guides. We went to several of the famous tourist spots, including the Eiffel Tower and the Louvre Museum.

On the way back to the hotel, we discovered a wonderful French bakery. We actually smelled the aroma from the bakery before we found it. Someone said, "What is that amazing smell?", and we all agreed and started looking around. It turned out to be a fantastic bakery shop a few doors down from where we were standing. We went in and finished the night with wine and delicious French pastries.

The third night took a turn of its own as Miss Colleen and I went on a romantic evening, just the two of us. We used our time to visit several small shops and a few art galleries. The weather was warm, with a slight breeze, and very pleasant, so we boarded a small boat and sailed along the River Seine. During the day, the river was dirty-looking, but at night, it turned into a magical place. The sound of water lapping the sides of the boat was very soothing, and the lights of the city played on the ripples in the water like fairies dancing to a constantly changing tune.

Afterward, we realized we were not far from our hotel and decided to walk back. There were not many people out, but the neighborhood was good, and the streets were well lit.

Two blocks from the hotel, my instincts went on high alert. The upcoming block was dark because a streetlight had been broken. The fact that it had been broken and not burned out added to my concern. It turned out that my concerns were justified. As we approached an alleyway, two thugs jumped out in front of us. One was holding what appeared to be a gigantic knife. I am sure the circumstances made the knife appear much larger than it actually was. I tried to seem more frightened than I was in hopes of throwing the knife-holder off guard. When I was ready, I made a little head fake. This caused the person with the knife to swing at me. Since I anticipated it, I was able to sidestep the swing. I grabbed the person's wrist and gave it a sharp twist. This brought his elbow up and out, facing me. I drove the palm of my free hand at and through his elbow. With his arm now separated, he fell to the ground, screaming. As he went down, I reached across him and drove my thumb into the eye of his partner, who also fell to the ground, holding his eye and screaming in pain. I took Miss Colleen's hand, and we proceeded to our hotel at a much faster pace than before.

The next morning, at breakfast, I told the team about our adventure. After that incident, anyone traveling to and from the hotel took a taxi.

At breakfast, and in spite of my repeated request not to, Miss Colleen insisted on telling everyone how amazing it was when I swung into action and what a hero I was.

FIFTEEN

THE LAST NIGHT of the conference was quiet. Everyone packed and retired early in preparation for their flights home the next day. We agreed to reconvene in Washington, D.C., in two weeks.

Returning to my quarters in D.C., I found a few phone messages waiting. There was only one of any importance. It was from Senator Noland. He said he was giving a fundraising speech at a particular hotel the following Tuesday at 2:00 PM. We could meet there for lunch and discuss whatever I had in mind. I called his office and confirmed the meeting.

The next item was to call the president and give him a recap of the conference. I also invited him to attend the next team meeting. I thought it would be better for him to hear the team's views and concerns raised at the conference directly from them. The president wanted to attend but could not make it as scheduled, so we moved the meeting to the following week. The president invited us to meet at the White House, and I accepted. The next order of business was to notify the team of the change of plans. I advised them to think about summarizing their thoughts on the conference for the president. As part of that process, I asked them to preview in their minds questions the president might have for them.

Having advised the team, I decided to take my own suggestion and focus on my reactions to the conference. My realization from the conference was that all nations were intertwined in suffering from the effects of global warming. Global warming affected all the Earth's population. For instance, take the issue of fossil fuels like gasoline. One goal in fighting warming was to reduce carbon emissions caused by burning gasoline. The reduction would come with its own problems. Any significant reduction in usage would bring major financial loss to the oil-producing countries and bring the rest of the world with them.

Many countries were sitting on vast deposits of coal, which they used to produce power to run their industries. Those countries simply did not have the money or technology to switch to low-carbon emission options. In some countries, the problems were so severe that they seemed immune to solutions and could leave a person wanting to give up. For example, the degree of flooding and drought in some countries, and yes, some countries had both in the same year. That was the situation in many African countries.

In some of those countries, thousands of people died a year because of global warming events. I had noticed that in industrial nations, loss was largest in the area of material goods. There were deaths, but compared to some countries, that loss was very small. In some cases, comparing undeveloped nations to developed ones was comparing thousands of lives lost versus thousands of dollars lost. Because of that, I concluded that solving the problems caused by global warming in developed countries was easier than in undeveloped ones. It was simply easier to solve problems of property damage than the loss of life caused by hunger, flood, and drought. Attending the conference made me want to renew my efforts toward fighting the global warming challenges.

When the president met with the team, their feedback closely matched mine. Several team members expressed concerns relative to their areas of expertise. The team entomologist was concerned with the way the insects were deserting areas of drought, and our zoologist, Suzan Sanders, was concerned with the change in habitats of the African Plains animals.

After hearing of the problems of the African nations, the president said, "I am going to ask the Secretary of State to look into forming a team like ours among African nations."

With that, the team meeting concluded.

I spent the next few days relaxing, visiting old friends, and just enjoying Washington. Then, it was time to meet with Senator Noland. As I entered the hotel and headed for the dining room, I passed the lounge. It was dimly lit, and I almost missed spotting our team entomologist, Dr. Milton. I stepped in to say hello and ask what brought him to Washington.

He seemed glad to see me but not surprised. He said, "I am at the headquarters of the National Geographic Society to discuss writing an article on the movement of killer bees into the United States."

We visited for a few more minutes, and I moved on to my meeting with the senator.

Senator Noland greeted me with that firm and friendly handshake that I had come to expect from senators. We had a pleasant lunch, and I told him about the international conference the team had attended. He seemed very interested; his attention never wavered and only shifted when he interrupted to ask a pointed question.

After some additional small talk, I moved directly onto the subject of the meeting. I told him, "I am tying up some loose ends from the murder investigation of Edward La Mount. Specifically, I am interested in the meetings between you and La Mount and why the meetings were never mentioned to the team."

The senator said he had been impressed with La Mount's idea of slowing funding to end global warming until there was an established target to indicate success. He said, "Based on our talks, I am considering having my committee reduce or redirect the funds for combatting global warming. I can think of two reasons why La Mount did not discuss our meeting with your team. One, on several occasions, he had expressed his views to the team, and two, our conversations had nothing to do with the function of the team."

I thanked the senator for his time and told him my curiosity had been satisfied. Rising to leave, the senator stood with me and said, "It is a while before my speech, and I will walk you out."

Passing the lounge, I looked to see if Milton was still there, and he was not. I asked the senator if he had seen him, and he said, "I did not but wish I had. I would have liked to have said hello."

We stood on the sidewalk and engaged in polite conversation. As we were talking, I noticed a car careen around the far corner, coming toward us at high speed. As the car got closer, I saw a gun protruding from the car's rear window. I threw my body onto the senator's, and we fell to the ground as a whistling of gunshots sailed over our heads.

I raised my head in time to see the car make a sharp right turn at the corner. My sixth sense told me it would make another right at the next block, and that would lead to the bridge, taking the assailants out of Washington and into Virginia for an escape.

I got to my feet and raced toward the alley across the street.

My hope was that I could intercept the car as it came down the next street over. Just before I exited the alley, I noticed a trash can sitting by a doorway. I grabbed it and dragged it with me.

My timing was almost perfect, as the car approached me just as I exited the alley. With all my strength, I threw the trashcan at the car's windshield. It was as good a pitch as any professional ball player had ever thrown. The windshield completely shattered, and the driver lost control of the car and smashed into the side of a building.

I ran toward the car, withdrawing my weapon as I ran. A person emerged from the backseat of the car and turned his weapon in my direction. I rapped off two shots before he fired, and both hit within the area of his heart. He fell back into the car, no longer with the living. The driver took a shot out the car window and missed. I fired three shots in return. One hit the doorframe, and the other two were headshots right on target, and the driver joined his friend in nowhere land.

The police arrived on the scene very quickly, and after a brief conversation in which I gave them my contact information, I hurried back to check on the senator. Approaching the front of the hotel, I noticed Dr. Milton entering a cab midway down the block. I thought he had left the hotel earlier and made a mental note of him hanging around until later. The senator seemed okay, with the exception of his clothing, which was a little misaligned from being thrown to the ground. He was surrounded by police, onlookers, and several press members who were there to cover his fundraising speech. I waved goodbye to him and headed back to my base.

SIXTEEN

THE FOLLOWING DAY, I was shocked at the headlines carried by most of the local newspapers: "Assassination Attempt on President's Special Investigator." It never occurred to me that I was a target. The senator was on the Senate Intelligence and Armed Forces committees, and it seemed to me that he would be the natural target. When reading the newspaper, it was clear the senator had made the conclusion about me being the target and said so to the press, who bought into his conclusion. They went on to speculate that I was the target because I was getting close to solving Professor La Mount's murder. It had not occurred to me. Did someone think I knew something I did not? I still thought of the senator as the target, but I definitely had something new to consider.

The assassins were Arabic but had no terrorist connections, which might have been suspected. The FBI determined it was not a terrorist attack but could come up with no good motive. One of the assassins had been a suspect in two prior murders but had not been tried due to lack of evidence.

After the incident, things settled down, and I tried to put recent events out of my mind and just enjoy being alive. It was spring, and I was in one of the greatest cities for springtime: Washington, D.C., which kicked off springtime with the Cherry Blossom Festival. The diameter of the Tidal Basin was lined completely with cherry trees in full bloom. Their white and pink petals combine to produce one of nature's most beautiful displays. The appearance of the blossoms is closely followed by the manifestation of tourists from throughout the country, and the blossoms do not disappoint. The city is also filled with great museums, cultural events, and art galleries. There are monuments to great leaders and others intended to honor the men and women who gave their lives defending our freedom. When I visit the war memorials, I am always filled with pride to be part of the United States Military. Most major nations in the world have embassies in Washington, D.C., and throughout the year, they hold parties and events to celebrate their own national holidays. On any given day, the city is filled with soldiers, tourists, diplomats, and average citizens from all over the world.

When spring turns to summer, the same conditions exist, but the atmosphere slows down. The temperature and humidity go up, and the pace slows down, but it is still the same great city.

During the spring and summer, our team meetings continued, but they held a lighter feeling than when conducted in the dead of winter. Everyone dressed in brighter colors and talked more about events they had attended or the flowers in their garden.

During the spring, the relationship between Miss Colleen and I grew. Neither of us was ready for it to become too serious, but it was a caring and supportive relationship.

My joy over the seasons ended suddenly one day late in summer. I had gone to the base gym to work out and shower. Upon returning to my room, I turned on the television and was shocked by the lead story: "Senator Drake of Texas found dead of apparent suicide." The story went on to say that the police had found a note but were not releasing the contents. A neighbor had become concerned about the senator and called the local security company that patrolled the housing development. They went in and found the body hanging from a rafter. I tried to get dressed quickly but kept stopping to think over what had just happened. I knew the senator was in a down place because of his wife's passing, but nothing to this level.

While I finished getting dressed, the phone rang, and it was the president.

He asked, "Have you heard about Senator Drake?", and, I said I had.

The president said, "I knew the senator and his wife, and I am startled that he took his own life. I knew he was despondent over her death, but she had fought her illness for a long time. I would have thought he would have come to terms with the inevitable long before it happened. I am not very familiar with the rest of the family, but I do want to talk to them.

"Before I do, I would like to know a little more about what happened. I am asking you, as a favor, to find out what you can about what took place. Talk to the police and the neighbor. If you get into the house, see if you find anything that might help me relate to the family better."

I responded, "I will be happy to see what I can find out." I then went on to say, "This is going to be similar to when I asked questions about Edward La Mount's death. Several people would not talk to me, feeling my military police status gave me no authority in civilian crimes, but I will do what I can."

I finished getting dressed and headed for the police station serving the area where the senator lived. I had a bit of luck there. They recognized me from the newspaper and knew I worked for the president. Because of that, they were willing to share what they knew. They had been called by the security company and arrived shortly after. They found the senator hanging from the rafter dressed as if going to work. He was in shoes, socks, slacks, and a dress shirt. It looked like he had just finished a cup of coffee. The senator left a note, but the police no longer had it.

Shortly after their arrival, the FBI arrived and took over the investigation, which is apparently normal procedure in deaths—other than natural causes—of high-ranking government officials. I called the FBI and was told they could not discuss an ongoing investigation.

My next step was to go to the senator's house and interview the neighbor who originally called the security company with his concerns. His name was George Stone. When we met, he was dressed casually but nicely and was very friendly. He said he was sixty-six years old and retired. He was heavyset, balding, and appeared distraught over the senator's death. They had been friends for several years and had developed a habit of meeting at the local coffee shop every Monday and Friday. They would meet about eight in the morning before the senator went to work and George headed home to his garden.

That particular morning, the senator had not shown. George assumed he had an early meeting and had gone straight to work. However, when George got home, the senator's car was sitting in the driveway. Thinking the senator might have overslept or been sick, George decided to check. He forcefully knocked on the door several times with no response. He then used his cell phone to call several times, and again, no response. At that point, George became quite concerned and called the local security company that paroled the neighborhood. They found the senator's body dangling from where he had taken his last breath.

I asked George, "Did you see the scene yourself?", and he said, "I did."

My next question was, "Did you notice anything about the hanging that looked unusual?"

He responded, "I hate to admit it, but yes, I did. I noticed the rope itself was brand-new as if he had bought it just for that purpose."

I thanked George for his time. It was getting toward evening, so I grabbed some dinner and headed back to base. There, I settled down to watch a baseball game on television. The third inning had just started when the phone rang. It was the president. He asked if I could come to the White House the next morning at nine o'clock.

I said, "Yes, sir. What's up?"

He said, "I don't have time to talk about it right now, but it will be quite clear when I see you tomorrow."

With that, we said goodbye, and I went back to my baseball game.

SEVENTEEN

THE NEXT MORNING, I walked into the Oval Office at 9:00. As usual, I was overcome by my surroundings and the realization that I was talking to the man the country elected to represent them to the world. The president was standing there with a man who looked familiar, but I could not place him.

The president said, "Good morning, Major. Let me introduce John Victor, director of the Federal Bureau of Investigation. He will tell you why he is here."

As soon as the president introduced him, I recognized him from many television news broadcasts. He looked thin on television and even thinner in person. His body seemed relaxed, but his eyes scanned me for clues as to what I might be thinking.

The director began, "Good morning, Major. The president explained that he asked you to investigate several recent events. He also said you are having difficulty because people do not recognize your authority in civilian matters. After talking to the president and reviewing your personnel file, I think I have a solution. I am here to give you the proper oath of office. I will then hand you the badge and identification identifying you as a special agent of the Federal Bureau of Investigation. This will give you authority in civil matters and access to all the bureau's resources."

I was shocked and overcome by the power just given me. Both the president and Mr. Victor indicated that they needed to get back to work, so I again thanked them and headed out.

Once away from the White House, I wasted no time in using my newfound status. I headed straight for the headquarters of the Federal Bureau of Investigation. There, I asked for the agent in charge of the senator's investigation. I was directed to the desk of Agent Bill Baxter. I was not sure what kind of reception I would receive. Yes, I now had the authority, but I could still be an outsider poking my nose into Bill's case.

When I met Bill, I was quite pleased. He had been advised about my coming and was very receptive to my presence. He had been with the agency for a little over twenty years and had gotten past being overly protective.

He said, "I am working several other cases and welcome any additional help." Bill suggested we start by looking at the evidence that had been collected.

We started with the photos of the suicide scene. They were pretty much as expected, taken in the living room with its high-vaulted ceiling and open beams. The senator had managed to get a rope tied around one of the beams. The other end was drawn tight around the senator's throat. The step stool he used had been kicked over and lay on its side a foot or so away.

The next item was the note. It had fingerprints on it, but they were too smudged to be used. The note read, "I can no longer go on facing the loss of my wife and my integrity. Thanks to all who supported me through it all." It was signed Donald, not Don. I guess he thought the note was formal enough to require his actual name and not a nickname. We had no idea what "loss of my integrity" meant, but the loss of his wife seemed motivation enough. After all, how many reasons does one need to commit suicide?

The next thing we looked at was a ledger of expenses. It was an account of all expenses incurred due to his wife's illness. There were many, and most were quite large—lengthy hospital stays, expensive (regular and experimental) drugs, and consultations with medical specialists. There was one entry labeled Washington First National Bank. Under it, several deposits of $25,000 were listed and referenced as loans. Later, there were sales of stocks used to pay back the loans. More recently, there were several more deposits of $25,000, assumed to be additional bank loans. One thing was clear—the wife's medical expenses had not decreased even toward the end.

As Bill and I looked over the ledger, we both noticed something and shared it with each other. The writing in the ledger appeared slightly different from the writing in the suicide note. The difference was so slight it was hard to say it was different. Some of the letters in the note had a stronger slant to the left than in the ledger. It was not such a big difference that you could say it was written by a different person. It could simply be the amount of time between writing the ledger and writing the note. It could also be the emotional impact of writing a suicide note. Regardless of the reason, we made a note of it in our written report. If need be, we could have a handwriting expert look at it later.

I thanked Bill for being so kind in accepting me as a partner. I told him, "I will go by Washington First National Bank to review some of the ledger entries and then head home."

At the bank, I showed my new credentials and was directed to the office of Harry Watson, the chief operation officer. The bank officer was friendly and very willing to cooperate. The bank records confirmed the loans and their repayment. The records, however, showed no recent loans associated with the $25,000 deposits. The deposits appeared not to be loans at all.

This brought to mind the phrase in the note, "loss of integrity." Could the deposits be a bribe? If yes, what for?

I asked to see photos of the checks used for the deposits. It took a few minutes to locate them. As I talked to Harry, a bank clerk entered and handed Harry several sheets of paper. They were photocopies of the checks, which he handed to me. They were written to an organization named "To Those in Need." They, in turn, were funded through a trust fund set up by Trikeco Construction. To Those in Need's motto was, "Unsecured loans to those of high achievement." It sounded to me like a company set up to give out money it never expected to get back.

I notified the president and the FBI of my findings and suspicions. I then started my own inquiry into what Senator Drake might have been involved in that would be worth a bribe. I only found one thing, and it started at about the same time as the deposits. The senator had fought hard to get a piece of legislation through Congress. It allowed the leasing of a large section of a national forest to a private company. The thing that made the deal unusual and hard to get through Congress was that it gave the mineral rights to the leasing company. That was always a hard sell because it meant partial destruction of the natural beauty of the area. The lease area was in a forest range in Montana, and the congressmen from that state had come together to fight the bill. Senator Drake had finally managed to get the bill passed after making many deals and promises and calling in a large number of favors.

The icing on the investigation cake came when I discovered the leasing company was Trikeco Construction. A little more inquiry revealed that Trikeco was already working the land. I decided to go to the source to find out what was going on. I would go to the operation site in Montana.

EIGHTEEN

I FLEW into Billings and rented a car for the hundred-and-twenty-mile drive to the site. It was a wonderful drive, going through miles of beautiful forest and surrounded by snow-capped mountains on all sides. The air was clear and clean. Occasionally, I would see one of several kinds of wild animals. It made me think if Montana were not so cold in the winter, it would be an exceptional place to live.

I started seeing signs saying, "Private Property Ahead—No Trespassing."

Finally, turning a corner, I went from beautiful forest to what looked like total devastation. The trees were gone, replaced by huge earth-moving equipment. It appeared to be a very large strip-mining operation. It made me wonder for a moment which was worse for the environment, man or climate change. I drove through the gate and parked in front of a large and new-looking trailer that appeared to be the command center. Inside, I met a man who introduced himself as Jack Twain, the site manager. I introduced myself and showed him my credentials.

He said, "We did not expect a government inspection so soon."

I replied, "This is not an official inspection; I am just curious as to what was being mined."

He said, "This is the only known large deposit of lithium in the United States. It is the main element used in producing long-lasting batteries. Currently, China is the world's leading producer of both lithium and lithium batteries. Lithium has become a very valuable commodity as the production of electric cars ramps up. An electric car company in the United States owning such a property would save huge sums of money by making their own batteries."

I agreed and asked if I could have a tour of the site. It was an impressive operation, with large machines working in very organized patterns so as not to miss any area. I left understanding why someone would pay a hefty bribe to get the rights to it.

Flying back to Washington, I relaxed, reading an architectural magazine that showed pictures of various living room designs. The picture in the magazine and the picture of the suicide scene connected in my mind. I suddenly realized why the suicide photo did not feel right.

As soon as I landed, I picked up my car and headed for the senator's house. On the way, I stopped at a hardware store and purchased a tape measure, which I would need to check what I now suspected.

In the background of the suicide photo, there was a clock just a few feet below the ceiling peak. The noose appeared just slightly below that or about nine and a half or ten feet from the floor. Upon entering the house, I found and measured the step stool. It was three feet tall. To that, I added the senator's height of five feet, five inches. The distance of the noose from the floor and the senator's height plus the step stool's height was a difference of least a foot. There was no way the senator could have gotten his neck through that noose. This realization just moved things from suicide to murder.

I contacted Bill at the FBI and shared my conclusions. He came to the house, verified what I found, and agreed with me about the death being a murder. After that, the investigation turned in a new direction. The house was in a very nice neighborhood and had traffic cameras on almost every street. We looked at the cars parked on the street at the approximate day and time of death. We then ran the license plates. All matched local residents, with the exception of two. One was from West Virginia, and the owner was visiting a relative. The other was from Arizona. Upon further checking, the car was registered to Alliance Auto.

NINETEEN

THE CAMERA SHOWED MORE than just a parked car; it showed a man exiting the car, and even though you could not see his face, the body looked a lot like Alliance's head of security, Jason Aba. He appeared to be carrying a rope. We really got lucky with Senator Drake's doorbell camera. It was the most advanced model, with an accessory that recorded up to two weeks of images. Bill had the bureau's forensic team look at the doorbell. They were able to pull images of Jason Aba ringing the bell and entering the house.

I went back to the hardware store and talked to the clerk. He knew the senator and did not remember him buying any rope. I asked him to look to see if anyone had recently purchased rope.

He looked at his receipts, and I saw his eyebrows raise. He said, "Yes! Someone did, and I remember because the purchase was made using a check with the Alliance Auto Logo on it." He had never seen one of those before.

That same day, we issued an arrest warrant for Jason Aba. He was arrested the next morning as he pulled into his parking spot at work, and the arrest went smoothly. Two agents approached from either side as he exited his car. They each grabbed an arm and forced him over the hood of the car as they cuffed him. The whole thing took less than five minutes. Even after the arrest, our investigation continued. We talked to the senator's secretary and showed her Jason's photograph.

She identified him as a man who had delivered several packages to the senator at about the same time the deposits were made to his account. She said, "I assumed Mr. Aba was just another lobbyist."

Within an hour of the arrest, Jason's boss, Mr. William Sterns, was on the phone. He said he was shocked that Jason could have done such a thing.

When I asked if he had any idea why Jason would have done it, Sterns said, "The senator had toured the plant recently, and he and Jason had gotten into a heated argument over the United States' involvement in European conflicts. Ever since then, Jason had been fearful that the senator would block his citizenship application, and that was extremely important to Jason. I can't believe that would be a reason to kill someone, but who can account for the workings of the human mind?"

Sterns asked that I keep him informed as things developed. He managed to avoid implicating himself in the situation. The fact remained—Mr. Sterns was the only person who could have authorized checks written from the Trikeco Trust to Senator Drake. If Sterns was directly involved in bribing the senator, could he be involved in the murder of Edward La Mount? I kept that thought to myself but developed a plan to check it out.

I decided that after the next team meeting, I would make it a point to stay after everyone had left. My intention was to remove two of Mr. Sterns' cigarette butts from the ashtray and have the DNA from them compared to the DNA from the hair found in La Mount's hand. If they matched, I thought we had found our killer. At the end of our next meeting, I started to put my plan into action. As people were leaving, I fussed with my papers as if arranging them before placing them into my briefcase. This was to allow everyone to depart and leave the room to me.

Once the room was clear, I started with my plan. However, I failed to notice Sterns had forgotten and left his briefcase in the corner of the room. Just as I was picking butts out of the ashtray and putting them into a plastic bag, Sterns returned for his briefcase. When he saw what I was doing, there was a blank stare and a moment of bewilderment. Then, Sterns realized what I was doing and why. His eyes narrowed. His face went red, and his fist tightened until his knuckles went white. Without hesitation, and in a moment of furry and rage, he charged, with his cane raised high as if to smash my skull. I met his charge with my own. I drove my shoulder into his midsection. The cane's head landed on the left side of my back, causing a great deal of pain. My charge sent both of us to the floor. Despite the pain, I got to my feet first, and as he struggled to get to his feet, I delivered a roundhouse kick to the side of his head. He collapsed as if someone had just turned off his switch. As he lay there, I used our belts to hog-tie him. When he came to, I arrested him for assaulting a federal officer.

When his DNA proved to be a match, murder was added to the charge. Both Aba and Sterns made interesting legal moves. Both made deals to take the death penalty off the table in exchange for testifying against the other. Later, each was convicted of murder and given a life sentence.

TWENTY

THE MURDER of La Mount had been to prevent him from convincing Congress to cut spending on such items as electric cars. The assassination attempt on Senator Noland was for pretty much the same reason. Senator Noland liked La Mount's idea of establishing goals before spending more money on solutions. He was considering having his committee reduce the amount of money they would allocate to electric car production. Such a move would have cost Mr. Sterns millions in personal wealth and loss of industry leadership. As it turned out, the only reason Edward Milton was around after the assassination attempt on Senator Noland was his inability to hail a cab any sooner.

As far as Senator Drake was concerned, his conscience had started bothering him after his wife's death, and he'd tried to return what was left of the bribe money. That alerted Sterns to the fact that Drake could go public with a confession at any time and destroy everything. With such a possibility, the senator had to go. Sterns had paid Aba a large sum of money plus company stock to do the job. He might have gotten away with it had it not been for my reading an architectural magazine on my flight back from the Trikeco lithium site.

As painful as my back injury caused by Sterns' gold-headed cane was, it was well tended to by Miss Colleen. Although I am certain her treatment techniques were not medically approved, they certainly took my mind off the pain.

A week after the trials of Sterns and Aba, the president sent for me.

Once in the Oval Office and seated, the president said, "Well, Major, it certainly has been a few action-packed months for you. How are you feeling?" Before I could answer, he continued, "I noticed your back is still bothering you. I can tell by the way you are walking."

I said, "Yes. Sterns got me pretty good with his cane."

The president said, "I called you to the office because I want you to take a week off and go somewhere for some realization. That way, you will come back fully refreshed and ready to go."

I responded, "I agree; I could use a break, and you do not have to make that offer twice. Your comment about 'coming back fully refreshed and ready to go' reminded me of something I have been wanting to discuss with you."

The president smiled and asked, "What would that be, Major?"

"Mr. President, the work of the Global Warming Committee has stabilized. We now only meet on the second Tuesday of each month. If anything needs attention between meetings, we handle it over the phone or via television conference. My point is, I am not using very much of my time on committee work. I feel you are not using my time for your best interest."

The president's forehead wrinkled slightly. He leaned forward in his chair and looked directly at me. He said, "Let me make this perfectly clear—I want the committee's work to continue, and you are part of that. I do understand what you are saying, and I do have some things in mind for you. I am putting together a group to look at the possibility of replacing the hole in the ozone layer with man-made ozone. You recall that was an idea that came out of the committee you are on. I want you to be involved in that effort.

"In addition, now that you are a member of the Federal Bureau of Investigation, feel free to assist them with any investigation they need help with. Be assured that I am not going to waste valuable skills like yours. I would not be much of an executive if I did that, would I?"

We shook hands. I thanked the president for his time. I assured him I would pick the dates for my vacation and let him know.

I left the Oval Office and headed for my office at the White House. As soon as I reached my office, I called Miss Colleen and asked, "Can you get time off and go with me for a week in the Caribbean?"

Two weeks later, we were off to a beach resort for fun and relaxation. I did return refreshed and ready for whatever came next.

ABOUT THE AUTHOR

Forney Shell holds a Bachelor's degree in Business Management and a Master's degree in Human Resource Management. Forney retired for Boeing Aircraft with the title of Senior Research Design Engineer and contributed his designs to the Space Shuttle and Moon lander. He is the owner of Pan Piper Travel and has been in the travel industry for twenty-one years. He is a former professor at the college of business and Technology in Charlottesville, Virginia. Forney is regularly invited to speak at clubs and civic groups.

Forney is the author of two nonfiction books, *Mastering the Bucket List: From Planning to Action* and *Having a Successful Life: No Permission Needed*. *The Global Warming Murders* is Forney's first novel.

www.ingramcontent.com/pod-product-compliance
Lightning Source LLC
Chambersburg PA
CBHW040544170726
48295CB00012B/585